MOTHER GOOSE

Mother Goose

A Collection of Classic Nursery Rhymes

SELECTED AND ILLUSTRATED BY

Michael Hague

Henry Holt and Company
New York

Special thanks to the children of the Colorado Springs School

Henry Holt and Company, Inc.
Publishers since 1866
115 West 18th Street
New York, New York 10011

Henry Holt is a registered
trademark of Henry Holt and Company, Inc.

Published in Canada by Fitzhenry & Whiteside Ltd.,
195 Allstate Parkway, Markham, Ontario L3R 4T8.

Library of Congress Cataloging-in-Publication Data
Mother Goose
Mother Goose: a collection of classic nursery rhymes.
Summary: A noted contemporary artist presents a large
selection of Mother Goose rhymes.
1. Nursery rhymes. [1. Nursery rhymes] I. Hague,
Michael. II. Title.
PZ8.3.M85Hag 1984 398′.8 83-22559
ISBN: 0-8050-0214-6

Printed in Mexico
on acid-free paper. ∞

11   13   15   17   19   20   18   16   14   12

To Judy Noyes and all her grandchildren

PREFACE

Until very recently I believed that Mother Goose was indeed a real person who lived a long time ago in a country across the sea. I assumed that her house was in one of those villages where all of the roofs are thatched.

However, many scholars will tell you that there never was a *real* Mother Goose. Other scholars will insist that the rhymes in the collection actually represent some sort of political satire. Perhaps they are right, but I feel that any serious reader of Mother Goose should immediately dismiss such notions. In all the years that the rhymes have been read and sung no child has questioned them or asked what they really mean.

I have always known how I would illustrate each Mother Goose rhyme. After all, the pictures were implanted in my mind's eye many years ago. To those who lack the uneducated eyes of a child my pictures may seem too literal and full of superfluous detail. But to me and, I hope, to my readers they are just the opposite: They represent the realm of a child's imagination, where anything is possible. The domain of Mother Goose is not one of concrete images, fixed and immovable. Rather, it is a place where the real mixes with the not so real. If you could look inside your child's mind, it would look like the inside of his or her toybox; every nook and cranny is packed with little details, and not one of them is extraneous or out of place.

I have come to realize that the Mother Goose rhymes were not meant just for children. They also speak to parents in a very special way. One of life's greatest pleasures is rocking your baby in your arms while softly chanting a Mother Goose rhyme. As your voice drops to a whisper and the baby falls asleep, the words become a gentle hum. Still humming the rhyme, you lay your child across your chest. It is difficult to let go of either the child or the rhyme, so you hold on to both of them as long as you can.

Yet there is also something bittersweet about singing your child to sleep with a rhyme. It feels good to cradle your baby in your arms and know that it is safe and sound, but it also feels a bit sad because you know that your child will grow up so soon and that you will never be able to do this again. My wife and I have had three little ones to sing rhymes to. I feel fortunate to have a baby right now as I am illustrating this book, for only through a child can the real Mother Goose come alive. When I am singing our new son, Devon, to sleep, I use the rhyme "Bye, baby bunting." If Devon is in the mood to go to sleep, it works very well. If not . . . I give him to his mother.

Illustrating this collection of rhymes has been especially pleasurable. I have not been afraid to be sweet, and I have had great fun. After all, Mother Goose is nonsense, and nonsense is fun.

MICHAEL HAGUE

MOTHER GOOSE

Oᴌᴅ Mother Goose,
    When she wanted to wander,
Would ride through the air
    On a very fine gander.

1

SEE-saw, Margery Daw,
Jacky shall have a new master;
Jacky shall have but a penny a day,
Because he can't work any faster.

J<small>ACK</small> Sprat could eat no fat,
His wife could eat no lean,
And so between them both, you see,
They licked the platter clean.

OLD King Cole
Was a merry old soul,
And a merry old soul was he;
He called for his pipe,
And he called for his bowl,
And he called for his fiddlers three.

Every fiddler, he had a fiddle,
And a very fine fiddle had he;
Twee tweedle dee, tweedle dee, went the fiddlers.
Oh, there's none so rare
As can compare
With King Cole and his fiddlers three.

MARY had a little lamb,
   Its fleece was white as snow;
And everywhere that Mary went
   The lamb was sure to go.

It followed her to school one day,
   That was against the rule;
It made the children laugh and play
   To see a lamb at school.

And so the teacher turned it out,
   But still it lingered near,
And waited patiently about
   Till Mary did appear.

"Why does the lamb love Mary so?"
   The eager children cry;
"Why, Mary loves the lamb, you know,"
   The teacher did reply.

POLLY put the kettle on,
Polly put the kettle on,
Polly put the kettle on,
    We'll all have tea.

Sukey take it off again,
Sukey take it off again,
Sukey take it off again,
    They've all gone away.

GREAT A, little a,
Bouncing B,
The cat's in the cupboard
And she can't see.

As I went to Bonner,
  I met a pig
  Without a wig,
Upon my word and honor.

11

HECTOR Protector was dressed all in green;
Hector Protector was sent to the Queen.
The Queen did not like him,
No more did the King;
So Hector Protector was sent back again.

DIDDLETY, diddlety, dumpty,
The cat ran up the plum tree;
  Half a crown
  To fetch her down,
Diddlety, diddlety, dumpty.

I saw three ships come sailing by,
  Come sailing by, come sailing by,
I saw three ships come sailing by,
  On New Year's Day in the morning.

And what do you think was in them then,
  Was in them then, was in them then?
And what do you think was in them then,
  On New Year's Day in the morning?

Three pretty girls were in them then,
    Were in them then, were in them then,
Three pretty girls were in them then,
    On New Year's Day in the morning.

One could whistle, and one could sing,
    And one could play on the violin;
Such joy there was at my wedding,
    On New Year's Day in the morning.

THERE was an old woman
Lived under a hill,
And if she's not gone
She lives there still.

LITTLE Tommy Tittlemouse
Lived in a little house;
He caught fishes
In other men's ditches.

JACK and Jill went up the hill
To fetch a pail of water;
Jack fell down and broke his crown,
And Jill came tumbling after.

Up Jack got, and home did trot,
As fast as he could caper,
And went to bed to mend his head
With vinegar and brown paper.

19

RUB-a-dub-dub,
Three men in a tub,
And who do you think they be?
The butcher, the baker,
The candlestick-maker,
Turn 'em out, knaves all three.

JACK be nimble,
Jack be quick,
Jack jump over
The candlestick.

BOBBY Shafto's gone to sea,
　　Silver buckles at his knee;
He'll come back and marry me,
　　Bonny Bobby Shafto!

Bobby Shafto's fat and fair,
　　Combing down his yellow hair;
He's my love for evermore,
　　Bonny Bobby Shafto!

HEY diddle diddle,
The cat and the fiddle,
The cow jumped over the moon;

The little dog laughed
To see such sport,
And the dish ran away with the spoon.

HICKORY, dickory, dock,
The mouse ran up the clock.
The clock struck one,
The mouse ran down,
Hickory, dickory, dock.

LITTLE Jack Horner
Sat in the corner,
Eating a Christmas pie;
He put in his thumb,
And pulled out a plum,
And said, "What a good boy am I!"

THE man in the moon
Came down too soon,
And asked his way to Norwich;
He went by the south,
And burnt his mouth
With supping cold plum porridge.

Humpty Dumpty sat on a wall,
Humpty Dumpty had a great fall.
All the king's horses,
And all the king's men,
Couldn't put Humpty together again.

Pussy cat, pussy cat, where have you been?
I've been to London to look at the queen.
Pussy cat, pussy cat, what did you there?
I frightened a little mouse under her chair.

LITTLE Miss Muffet
Sat on a tuffet,
Eating her curds and whey;
There came a big spider,
Who sat down beside her
And frightened Miss Muffet away.

Ride a cock-horse to Banbury Cross,
To see a fine lady upon a white horse;
Rings on her fingers and bells on her toes,
And she shall have music wherever she goes.

Bᴇ, baby bunting,
Daddy's gone a-hunting,
Gone to get a rabbit skin
To wrap the baby bunting in.

Boys and girls come out to play,
The moon doth shine as bright as day.
Leave your supper and leave your sleep,
And join your playfellows in the street.
Come with a whoop and come with a call,

Come with a good will or not at all.
Up the ladder and down the wall,
A half-penny loaf will serve us all;
You find milk, and I'll find flour,
And we'll have a pudding in half an hour.

DICKERY, dickery, dare,
The pig flew up in the air;
The man in brown soon brought him down,
Dickery, dickery, dare

Ring-a-ring o' roses,
A pocket full of posies,
A-tishoo! A-tishoo!
We all fall down.

THERE was an old woman who lived in a shoe,
She had so many children she didn't know what to do;

38

She gave them some broth without any bread;
She whipped them all soundly and put them to bed.

WEE Willie Winkie runs through the town,
Upstairs and downstairs in his nightgown,
Rapping at the window, crying through the lock,
"Are the children all in bed, for now it's eight o'clock?"

THREE blind mice, see how they run!
They all ran after the farmer's wife,
Who cut off their tails with a carving knife,
Did you ever see such a thing in your life,
    As three blind mice?

THERE was an old woman tossed up in a basket,
Seventeen times as high as the moon;
Where she was going I couldn't but ask it,
For in her hand she carried a broom.
"Old woman, old woman, old woman," quoth I,
"Where are you going to up so high?"
"To brush the cobwebs off the sky!"
"May I go with you?"
"Aye, by-and-by."

Pᴀᴛ-a-cake, pat-a-cake, baker's man,
Bake me a cake as fast as you can;
Pat it and prick it, and mark it with B,
Put it in the oven for baby and me.

I saw a ship a-sailing,
    A-sailing on the sea,
And oh but it was laden
    With pretty things for thee.

There were comfits in the cabin,
    And apples in the hold;
The sails were made of silk,
    And the masts were all of gold.

The four-and-twenty sailors,
    That stood between the decks,
Were four-and-twenty white mice
    With chains about their necks.

The captain was a duck
    With a packet on his back,
And when the ship began to move
    The captain said, "Quack! Quack!"

Rain, rain, go away,
Come again another day.

MARY, Mary, quite contrary,
How does your garden grow?
With silver bells and cockle shells,
And pretty maids all in a row.

LITTLE Boy Blue,
  Come blow your horn,
The sheep's in the meadow,
  The cow's in the corn;
But where is the boy
  Who looks after the sheep?

He's under a haycock,
  Fast asleep.
Will you wake him?
  No, not I,
For if I do,
  He's sure to cry.

49

HERE am I,
Little Jumping Joan;
When nobody's with me
I'm all alone.

DIDDLE, diddle, dumpling, my son John,
Went to bed with his trousers on;
One shoe off, and one shoe on,
Diddle, diddle, dumpling, my son John.

Hush-a-bye, baby, on the treetop,
When the wind blows the cradle will rock;
When the bough breaks the cradle will fall,
Down will come baby, cradle and all.

Hot cross buns!
Hot cross buns!
One a penny, two a penny,
Hot cross buns!
If your daughters do not like them
Give them to your sons.

Baa, baa, black sheep,
   Have you any wool?
"Yes, sir, yes, sir,
   Three bags full;
One for the master,
   And one for the dame,
And one for the little boy
   Who lives down the lane."

CURLY locks, Curly locks,
    Wilt thou be mine?
Thou shalt not wash dishes
    Nor yet feed the swine,
But sit on a cushion
    And sew a fine seam,
And feed upon strawberries,
    Sugar and cream.

LITTLE Tommy Tucker,
  Sings for his supper:
What shall we give him?
  White bread and butter.
How shall he cut it
  Without a knife?
How will he be married
  Without a wife?

ONE misty, moisty, morning,
When cloudy was the weather,
There I met an old man
Clothed all in leather;
Clothed all in leather,
With cap under his chin.
How do you do, and how do you do,
And how do you do again?

TWINKLE, twinkle, little star,
How I wonder what you are!
Up above the world so high,
Like a diamond in the sky.

INDEX OF FIRST LINES